W9-DID-451

Nothing but Nonsense

Columbus, OH • Chicago, IL • Redmond, WA

The McGraw-Hill Companies

The Independent Reading Books

The **Independent Reading Books** are reading books that fill the need for easy-to-read stories for the primary grades. The appeal of these stories will encourage independent reading at the early grade levels.

The stories focus on the Dolch 220 Basic Sight Vocabulary and the 95 Common Nouns. Beyond these lists, the books use about three new words per page.

This series was prepared under the direction and supervision of Edward W. Dolch, Ph.D.

This revision was prepared under the direction and supervision of Eleanor Dolch LaRoy and the Dolch Family Trust.

SRAonline.com

 SRA

Send all inquiries to:
SRA/McGraw-Hill
8787 Orion Place
Columbus, OH 43240-4027

Printed in the United States of America.

ISBN 0-07-602525-X

1 2 3 4 5 6 7 8 9 BSF 12 11 10 09 08 07 06 05 04

Table of Contents

2

The Bag

Once there was a grandmother called Sally who was very curious about all that went on around her. She was curious about the children who lived on her street, the squirrels that played in her grass, and the birds that lived in her trees. Sally was just curious!

One day an old grandfather walked down the street. He had a big, big bag. He came upon the grandmother.

He said, "Will you please take this bag to your house? But do not open it. I will come back for it."

"I will do what you say," said curious Sally. "I will take the big bag to my house, and I will not open it. I would never do that!"

But that day, as soon as the man had walked away, Sally opened the bag.

Many, many cats ran out of the bag. The cats ran around all day. Cats were on the grass. And cats jumped in the trees.

Sally wished she had not opened the bag. She did not know what to do.

Sally started to pick up the cats and put them back into the bag. How did the old man get so many cats into one bag?

Sally was growing tired of picking up cats. There were so many cats that she could not pick up them all.

When the sun went down, Sally was very tired. She went back to her house. The old grandfather was by her door.

"Where is the bag I gave you to keep for me?" asked the old man.

"Here it is," said a very tired Sally. How she wished she had not opened the bag and let out the cats.

"You have opened this bag!" said the old man. "Where are all the cats that I had in this bag?"

"The cats are on the grass. The cats are in the trees. All day long I have picked up cats and put them into the bag," said Sally. "But I cannot get all the cats back into the bag."

The man said, "Grandmother, you have spoiled my day and the day of many children.

"I was bringing these cats as a surprise to children who live where there are no cats. You have spoiled their surprise because you are so curious."

The old man started to walk away. But before he went, he said, "You will now be known as the woman who let the cats out of the bag."

To this very day, when a man or woman has spoiled a surprise of some kind, it is said that he or she "has let the cat out of the bag."

Why the Stork Has No Tail

One day the king of the storks called all the storks to him. The king of the storks said this to them:

"When I was little, I was put into a big box. A kind man came by and saw me in the box. 'No good man would box any bird,' he said. And he opened the box and let me out.

"I said to the kind man, 'You have helped me. Now when you want help, you will call me, and I will come to help you.'"

The king of the storks looked out at all the storks. Then he said to them, "The day has come, and that man has called for my help. And that is why I called you here on this day. Now I, your king, could use your help too."

"Today the kind man came to me," said the king. "He asked me to find for him a flower called the Red Wild Flower. This flower brings joy to those who see it. But the kind man does not know where to find this flower."

The king looked out at the storks.

"One of the children of this man is ill. She is so, so ill. The joy of the flower may help. If she sees it, she may get better. If not, she will always be ill and never know joy," the king said.

The storks looked down at the grass, not at the king.

"Is there one of you who knows where to find the Red Wild Flower?" asked the king.

The storks just looked down. Then one of the old, old storks came up to the king. One eye and one leg of this old stork were hurt.

"My good king," said the old stork, "when I was a boy, I flew to the Great Snapping Forest. There I saw the Red Wild Flower."

"In the Great Snapping Forest, there are trees that are like scissors," said the old stork. "One tree hurt my eye. One tree hurt my leg. If you go there, you must watch out for the trees. They are like scissors."

"Who will go to the Great Snapping Forest to find the Red Wild Flower?" asked the king of the storks.

All the storks looked at the old, old stork with a hurt eye and a hurt leg. Not one of the storks wanted to go to the Great Snapping Forest. Not one of the storks wanted to see the trees that are like scissors.

The king of the storks asked again, "Who will go and bring back the Red Wild Flower?"

Not one stork called out to help.

But then the old, old stork said, "I am very old, but I will help the king and the kind man. Let me go back to the Great Snapping Forest to find the Red Wild Flower."

"Old stork," said the king, "can you fly that far?"

"I can try," said the old stork.

And the old stork did. He flew far, far away. The old stork flew to where the big hills were. But he was so tired that he had to sit down on top of one of the big hills. When he was there, a little bird flew up to him.

"Go back," said the little bird. "The Great Snapping Forest will get you. Forget about going on."

"I hear you, but I cannot go back," said the old stork. "I must go on to the Great Snapping Forest. I have come to get the Red Wild Flower that grows on the floor of the Great Snapping Forest. I will tell you why."

And then the old stork did tell the bird about the king of the storks and the kind man.

"You must hear what I say," said the little bird. "Do not forget what I say to you. When the sun is over the tops of the trees, the trees sleep. They do not sleep very long. But when they sleep, you can get the Red Wild Flower from the floor of the Great Snapping Forest."

"I will not forget," said the old stork. "I hear what you say."

The little bird flew away. The old stork looked out from the hill.

The stork could see the Great Snapping Forest from the hill. When the sun was over the tops of the trees, the old stork flew to the Great Snapping Forest. He saw the Red Wild Flower. It was a joy to see! He picked it and flew back up over the trees.

The old stork did get the flower as the trees were sleeping. But he could not fly fast over the trees. The scissors of the trees started to open.

The old stork made it back to the king. He gave him the Red Wild Flower. It was a joy for the king to see. It would be a joy for the ill child.

But the other storks laughed. They laughed because the old stork had no tail!

As the old stork flew by one of the trees like scissors, one of the trees must have cut off his tail. But it did not hurt at all. His tail was just not there, but the ill child would have joy.

The king of the storks said to the other storks, "Why do you laugh at this old stork? He was willing to do what his king asked! And now he brings the Red Wild Flower so I may give it to the kind man to bring joy to his ill child."

But the old stork had no tail and the other storks just laughed and laughed.

As they laughed, the king flew very fast around them and cut their tails with scissors. The storks laughed so much that they did not see the fast king!

"Look at your own tails," said the king of the storks when he was done. "Look at your own tails!"

And every stork looked where its own tail had been. But not one stork had a tail.

And from that time to this, no stork has had a tail.

The Gentle People

Far, far away in the green, green hills, there lived a Gentle People. They very much liked the flowers and the birds and all the animals. The flowers, the birds, and the animals liked the people too.

The children of the Gentle People liked flowers, birds, and animals. The children were kind. They never hurt a flower or a bird or any animal. They wanted to be like the animals. They wanted to fly like the birds.

The king of the Gentle People would talk about what it was like to be an animal. It looked like he could talk to the animals and hear what they said.

The children would ask the king to talk to a bird. The children wanted to know what it was like to fly!

When the children would run in the green, green hills, it looked like they could hear the animals talk too. Could they?

The children did not know if they could hear the animals. They just ran and played. The animals sometimes looked as if they were playing the children's games.

Sometimes the children would play Mother May I. In the game, children would ask, "Mother, may I take a small jump to you?" The child who was "Mother" would sometimes say, "Yes, you may," or sometimes say, "No, you may not."

The first child to get to "Mother" then got to be "Mother" in a new game.

Upon the hill where the children ran and played, there lived many sheep. The sheep liked to eat the grass on the hill. Sometimes the children would play their game and the sheep would say, "Excuse us, but you are on our grass."

The children would keep right on playing. They did not think they could hear the sheep!

But the sheep would say once again, "Excuse us, but you are on our grass."

Then once, a child called Bianca did not keep playing the game. She did hear the sheep!

"Excuse me," Bianca said to a big sheep. "Did you just talk to us?"

"Yes, I did," said the big sheep. "You are playing on the grass we are trying to eat."

The child, Bianca, did not know what to do. The sheep did talk to her! What could a child say to a sheep?

"What is your name?" Bianca asked the big sheep.

"My name is Simon," said the sheep. "And you are on our grass."

"My name is Bianca. Why can the other children not hear you?" the child asked Simon.

"They can hear me," said Simon. "They just do not believe they can hear me. You are on our grass."

"Why cannot we play on your hill with all the grass?" asked Bianca.

"Because this hill is where we eat," said Simon. "You will hurt our grass."

"I see," said the child. "We will play over there, where there is no grass."

"Can I believe you?" asked Simon.

"You can play the game too," said Bianca. "Then you can watch over us and the other sheep."

"I believe that will work," said Simon, the sheep, to Bianca, the child.

Bianca called over to the other children and told them about her friend Simon, the sheep who could talk. Bianca told the other children that the sheep was their friend and that he would like to play the game with them.

Just then, it looked like the sheep started to talk to Bianca.

"What did the sheep say, Bianca?" the other children asked.

Bianca said, "This friend is Simon. Simon told me he does not like the name of the game we play. He does not think Mother May I is a good name because he is a father."

The children started to think.

Then one child said, "We can call the game 'Simon Says!'" And so it was.

And that is why today children play the game called Simon Says. The game is very much like Mother May I.

If you go far, far away to the green, green hills, you will always see one sheep looking over the other sheep and watching children play. The children will always be playing Simon Says.

If you do not believe that this is how it is, you can always go ask the sheep. He or she will tell you!

Why the Water Buffalo Has a Split Hoof

There once was a day when the animals would talk just as we do now. One day a turtle walking in the woods saw a water buffalo.

The turtle, which was very small, looked at the water buffalo, which was very big. The turtle could not help but think, "If I could just get this water buffalo to be my friend, I know that it could help me. It is so big, and I am so little."

"Good day to you, my friend," said the turtle to the water buffalo.

But the water buffalo did not talk to the turtle.

Then the turtle said to the water buffalo, "I think it is not good for me to live by myself. My good friend, will you come and live with me?"

The water buffalo had to stop. It looked at the turtle in the grass.

"Live with you?" said the water buffalo. "Why, I am a big water buffalo, and you are but a little turtle."

"I cannot help being little," said the turtle. "But I can think faster. And I can run faster too. Will you run with me to see who is faster?"

"What? A water buffalo run a race with a turtle?" said the water buffalo. And the water buffalo laughed and laughed.

"Well, if you will not run a race with me," said the turtle, "I shall tell all the animals in the woods that you are afraid. You are afraid to run a race with a turtle."

The water buffalo did not like this. It did not want all the other animals in the woods to think it was afraid of a turtle.

So the water buffalo said to the turtle, "I will run a race with you. We shall race over the road of the seven hills. And my legs will go up and down so fast that you will not see them. I will run over seven hills before you run over one hill." And the water buffalo ran off into the woods.

The turtle went to the woods. The turtle told some animals about the race with the water buffalo.

The turtle told many other turtles about the race with the water buffalo.

"If you will help me," it said to the turtles, "we can win this race. Then the animals in the woods will no longer laugh at turtles because we cannot run fast with our little legs. We will win this race."

The other turtles said they would help. So the turtle who was going to run the race asked seven turtles to go with it. They looked just like it did. The turtle showed them the road of the seven hills. On every hill, it put a turtle. It told the turtles just what to do to help it win.

On the day of the race, the turtle and the water buffalo went to the road of the seven hills. All the animals in the woods were there to watch the race.

"This is the day of the race," said the water buffalo. "And the animals will not forget seeing a water buffalo race with a turtle."

"Yes," said the turtle. "They will not forget this race. Let us be off."

They started off down the road of the seven hills. The water buffalo ran very fast. When it looked back, it could not see the turtle. But when it got to the top of the first hill, a turtle was on the hill.

"Here I am," called the turtle. "You must run faster to win this race."

The water buffalo ran, and each hoof was going faster. But at the top of Hill Two and Hill Three and Hill Four was a turtle.

Again, the water buffalo ran, each hoof going faster and faster. But at the top of Hill Five and Hill Six was a turtle. "Here I am," said the turtle each time. "You must run faster if you want to win this race."

And again, the water buffalo ran, each hoof going so fast that the animals could not see its legs. When it got to the top of Hill Seven, there was a turtle.

The water buffalo did not know how this turtle could run so fast. When the buffalo looked down, it looked at its hoofs. There was a split in each of its hoofs!

The turtle looked at the splits in the hoofs of the buffalo and said, "You ran so fast, you split your hoofs."

So to this day, that is why the water buffalo has a split in each hoof.

Why the Rooster Crows

A boy asked his grandmother, "Why does the rooster crow?"

The grandmother lived on a big farm. The boy would hear the rooster crow as the sun came up.

"Well, my boy, here is why I think the rooster started to crow," said Grandmother with a little laugh.

Grandmother then told this to the curious boy:

Once Rooster and Bear used to live here. Rooster was afraid Bear would eat him. But Rooster did not have to be afraid. Bear did not want to eat Rooster. Rooster did not know this, so he would sit in a tree and watch for Bear.

Now one day before the sun was up, Dog was out walking. She saw Rooster up in a tree. Dog walked by the tree again the day after that and the day after that. Rooster was always up in the tree.

"Why are you always up in that tree?" Dog asked Rooster.

"Because I do not want to get eaten by Bear," said Rooster. Then Rooster hid his head under his feathers.

Dog looked all around, but she did not see Bear. Dog had been walking around for many days, and she had not seen Bear at all.

"I have not seen Bear," said Dog.

"You cannot see him, but he is here," said Rooster. "He is watching. He comes out when the sun comes up. He would like to eat me then!" Rooster hid under his feathers again.

Dog walked away. She did not know much about Bear. But she did not think Bear wanted to eat Rooster. She looked back as Rooster hid under his feathers.

34

On the day after that, as the sun came up, Dog walked by Rooster in the tree again. Dog looked around but did not see Bear. Dog wished Rooster were not so afraid.

Dog walked and walked. On a road in the woods, Dog saw Bear. Dog was a little afraid, but she watched Bear walk around. Bear did not look hungry. So from far down the road Dog said, "Bear, when the sun comes up and you are hungry, would you eat Rooster?"

Bear looked at Dog. "Rooster? All those feathers!" said Bear. "I am never that hungry!"

"I was right," said Dog.

Dog was kind and did not like to see Rooster so afraid of Bear. How could Dog help Rooster? After thinking, she said to Bear, "Let us race. I think I am faster!"

"You? I do not think so," laughed Bear. With that, Bear started to run.

This is just what Dog wanted. She chased after Bear. Bear ran from Dog. Bear ran far and Dog chased him. Bear ran by Rooster in the tree. Dog chased after Bear. Rooster saw this. It looked like Bear was afraid of Dog!

The morning after that, Dog walked by Rooster in the tree. "Bear was afraid of you," said Rooster.

"That is right," said Dog. "Do not forget that. You can come down from the tree, and if you see Bear in the morning, just call me by my first name and Bear will run away."

"What is your first name, Dog?" asked Rooster.

"Cock-a-Doodle-Do," said Dog.

From that morning on, Rooster would call out "Cock-a-Doodle-Do! Cock-a-Doodle-Do!" if he saw Bear or not.

Then Grandmother said to the boy, "And that is why the rooster crows."

Just then, the sun came up, and the rooster on the farm started to crow like it always did.

"There he goes, Grandmother!" the boy said. "He is keeping that old bear away!"

Why Kangaroos Jump on Two Legs

Did you know that kangaroos did not always jump on two legs?

A long, long time ago kangaroos walked on four legs just like many other animals. Kangaroos did not walk well. They could not run fast. Many people do not know that. And people who did know once, now forget how kangaroos walked!

People forget, too, that a long, long time ago kangaroos were very curious. Kangaroos wanted to know about other animals and how they lived. Kangaroos hid in the woods, in the hills, and in the grasses and watched other animals.

After kangaroos saw what other animals did, they would try it too. So a long, long time ago you could hear kangaroos try to crow like a rooster or sing like a bird. You could see kangaroos try to go up a tree like a squirrel or in the water like a fish.

When kangaroos would do things like this, they looked very silly.

Kangaroos would pick up old feathers from the woods and put them on their backs to look like silly birds. Kangaroos would put little sticks on their heads to look like some cows. Time after time, kangaroos just looked very silly!

The animals kangaroos liked to watch best were people, like you and me. We may not think we are animals, but a long, long time ago kangaroos did.

Kangaroos would watch people do many things. Then kangaroos would try to do the things that people could do.

People could grow things. Kangaroos would try to grow things but could not. People could put up houses. Kangaroos would try to put up houses but could not. People could make fires. Kangaroos would try to make fires but could not.

The people and the animals did not know that kangaroos hid and watched them. They did not know that kangaroos were curious about what they did. And they did not know that kangaroos would try to do what they did.

When kangaroos could not do what animals or people could do, they were not happy. They would try and try, but they could never sing, go up trees, keep feathers on, put up houses, or do any of the things other animals and people could do. So kangaroos were never happy.

But kangaroos did not give up. And one day after the sun went down, the kangaroos hid in the woods as always and watched what people did. This time the kangaroos found two things they could do!

The people the kangaroos were watching had worked all day. Now they had found things to eat and had made a fire to keep warm.

The people were tired but did not want to go to sleep. So the people started to talk and sing.

Soon some of the people got up and started to jump around. The people looked happy.

The kangaroos watched and then said all at once, "We can do that!"

The kangaroos could hear the people talk.

"This is a silly dance, but I like it!" said a man.

"Me too," said a woman.

The kangaroos did not know what a dance was, but they did know what silly was.

"We can do this," said one of the kangaroos. "We are good at being silly."

One by one, the kangaroos stood up on their two back legs. After they stood up, one by one the kangaroos started to jump up and down on their back legs.

"Look, I can dance!" said one of the kangaroos.

"And you look silly. We all look silly, just like people. We can do two things people can do," said the kangaroos.

Soon all the kangaroos stood on their back legs and jumped up and down. They were happy!

The kangaroos' back legs were big and very strong. Their strong legs made the kangaroos jump higher and higher. Being happy helped the kangaroos jump higher too.

When the people saw the kangaroos, their singing came to a stop. They did not dance. The people just looked at the kangaroos doing their silly dance.

Then one boy started to laugh. Then all the people started to laugh. They laughed and laughed!

At first the kangaroos did not hear the people laugh. The kangaroos still jumped and jumped. But soon the kangaroos saw the people. This time the kangaroos were being watched! The kangaroos did not jump. They just stood still. They did not know what to do.

The people still laughed, and the kangaroos were afraid.

Then one of the kangaroos said, "Let us go!"

But the kangaroos did not run away on four legs. They jumped away on two legs! The kangaroos saw that they jumped faster on two legs. They were very surprised.

When the kangaroos were far away from the people, they came to a stop. The kangaroos all started to talk at once.

"We jump faster and run better on our back legs!" some of them said.

"We can dance and look silly like people!" said some of the other kangaroos.

From that day to this, kangaroos walk, run, and jump on their back legs. But what makes kangaroos very happy is still this: they can dance and look silly just like people.

Why Horses Cannot Write Stories

In the back of the barn, Harold the Horse walked up and down. He was not happy. "There are all these stories that tell about animals like sheep or water buffalo," he was thinking.

"There are stories about why storks do not have tails or why roosters crow or why kangaroos jump." He was thinking and thinking.

"Why are there no stories about an animal like me, a horse?" He said this, but no one could hear him. No other animals were in the barn.

"There are no stories that tell why a horse does this or looks like that," he said. "It is just not right!"

"What is not right?" asked Clare the Cow. Harold had not seen Clare walk into the barn.

Harold looked up. "I did not see you come in the barn, Clare," he said.

"What is not right?" asked Clare the Cow again.

"Well, that there are so many stories that tell why animals do this or look like that. But there are no stories that tell about horses and why they look like they do or do what they do!" said Harold.

"You may be right. I do not think I have read any," said Clare.

Harold stood still and looked at an old red wagon in the barn. Then he said to Clare, "I will write a story about horses!"

"That is a good idea," said Clare. "It could be a story like 'Why the Horse Walks on Two Legs.'"

"That is a silly idea," said Harold. "Horses do not walk on two legs. They walk on four."

"Just like cows and other animals," said Clare.

"There has to be a better idea for a story," said Harold.

"Yes," said Clare. "There has to be. How about 'Why Horses Have Little Tails'"?

"But horses do not have little tails," said Harold. "Look how big and full my tail is." Harold's tail went up and down.

Clare watched and said, "Well, then this idea might work. How about 'Why Horses Have Big and Full Tails'"?

"That is a good idea," said Harold. "What could I write?"

"Well, why *do* horses have big and full tails?" asked Clare.

Harold stood still again. "I do not know," he said. "We just have them."

"Then that might not be much of a story," said Clare.

"No, it might not be much of a story," said Harold.

Clare could tell Harold was not happy. "If we walk around the farm, we might think of an idea," she said.

"We might," said Harold. And they walked out of the barn.

After they walked a little, Clare said, "I think one of the best stories about animals is 'Why Zebras Have Stripes.'"

"That is a good story, and horses are like zebras, with no stripes," said Harold.

"You could write a story that tells why horses have no stripes," said Clare.

"What could I say?" asked Harold.

Clare had to think a little. Then she said, "You could say horses are not zebras so they do not have stripes."

Harold said, "That is not a good story idea."

Before Clare could talk again, Harold started to run around the farm. Clare chased after him. She could tell Harold was not happy at all.

Clare could not keep up with Harold. Clare was thinking how horses run so fast. That idea made her stop.

"Harold," Clare called. "I have a good idea! Harold, do you hear me?"

Harold called back. "I hear you, Clare." And he ran to her.

"Here it is," said Clare. "You could write a story that tells why horses are so fast."

"That is the best idea so far!" said Harold. "I know what I could write. Horses are so fast because they have long legs and are so strong."

Harold looked very happy as he told Clare this.

"Well, that is the real reason," said Clare. "But stories that tell why animals do this or look like that do not give the real reason."

"They don't?" asked Harold.

"No," said Clare. "Do you think storks do not have long tails because the king of storks cut off their tails with scissors?"

"No," said Harold.

"Or do you think the real reason a water buffalo has split hoofs is because of a race with a turtle?" asked Clare.

"No," said Harold.

"If you want the real reason for any of these things, you can look it up in books about real animals," said Clare.

"I get it. I have to make up a reason that tells why horses are so fast," Harold said.

"I think so," Clare said. "The story has to be from a long time ago too."

"So I cannot write a new story. I have to find an old story?" said Harold.

"No, you can write a new story. But you have to start by saying 'Once, a long time ago,'" said Clare.

That made Harold think. "What could I write then?" he asked.

Clare looked at Harold. "Are you trying to get me to do the work for this story?" she asked.

"No, I am just looking for a little help," said Harold.

Clare did some thinking and said, "You could write this: 'Once a long time ago, horses were small and weak, had little legs, and could not run fast.'"

Harold looked hurt. "Stop!" he said. "I could not write that."

"Why not?" asked Clare.

"Horses were small and weak and could not run fast? You cannot say those things about horses!" said Harold.

Clare said, "Those things are made up. It is only in the *story* that a long time ago, horses were small and weak and . . ."

"Stop! A story like that will hurt the feelings of horses," said Harold.

Clare could tell she had hurt Harold's feelings.

"Well, if it will hurt the feelings of horses, you cannot write it," said Clare.

"No, I cannot," said Harold.

"How about a story that says a long time ago horses had small teeth?" asked Clare.

"No!" said Harold.

"Big teeth?" asked Clare.

"No!" said Harold.

"No teeth?"

"No!"

"Were afraid?"

"No!"

"Were not afraid?"

"No!"

Clare started to laugh. Then Harold started to laugh too.

"Well, I think I cannot write a story about horses, Clare," said Harold. He was still laughing.

Clare was still laughing too but said, "I think I have a real idea, Harold. And it is a good one."

That made Harold stop laughing. "What?" he asked.

"The story would be called 'Why Horses Cannot Write Stories,'" said Clare.

At first, Harold looked like his feelings were hurt again. But then he started to laugh. "That would be a good story," he said.

Was it?

Why the Armadillo Has a Shell

A long, long time ago animals did not have coats of fur. So when it was cold, the animals were cold too. The animals could get very cold.

At first the animals did not know how to keep warm. Then they found an old loom. A loom can be used to weave coats.

Every one of the animals worked at the loom to weave a coat. Skunk made a coat of black and white fur. Lion made a coat of yellow fur. Rabbit made a coat of fur that was as white as snow. Bear made a coat of warm brown fur. Other animals made coats too.

Then the birds made coats. They made coats of feathers. Some of the birds' coats were red, yellow, blue, and green. Soon many animals came just to watch the birds make their coats on the loom.

After all the birds were done with their coats, the animals still watched to see who worked at the loom. They started to say which animals could weave well and which could not.

One of the first animals to weave a coat after the birds were done was Armadillo. He was afraid. He could tell that all the animals were now watching. Armadillo did not like to be watched.

As Armadillo started to weave, he saw all the animals' eyes watching him. At first Armadillo did well. He made the first part of his coat the right size.

But Armadillo could still see all the animals' eyes watching him. He looked at the animals so much that he did not see his own work. Armadillo did not know that the part of the coat he was working on was not the right size. When the other animals started to laugh, Armadillo looked to see what he had done. This part of the coat was too big!

Now Armadillo watched the loom—and only the loom—as he worked. He started to weave his coat in the right size again. Soon the coat was done.

When Armadillo put on the coat, the animals laughed again. The part of the coat by his head was the right size. The part of the coat by his tail was the right size. But the part of the coat over his back was too big! It not only looked like a big shell, but it was strong like a shell too.

The animals laughed and laughed at Armadillo. When they did, Armadillo hid his head and tail in the part of his coat that looked like a shell. And to this day, that is what Armadillo always does when he is afraid or is being watched.